DAT

THE SILVER WOOD

by DOUGLAS J. KIRBY
pictures by JENNY WILLIAMS

Published by Four Winds Press, a division of Scholastic Magazines, Inc., New York, N. Y., by arrangement with Constable Young Books Ltd., London. Originally published in England by Constable Young Books Ltd. First American edition 1967.

Text © 1966 by Douglas J. Kirby. Illustrations © 1966 by Jenny Williams.

FOUR WINDS PRESS □ NEW YORK

Printed in Great Britain by W. S. Cowell Ltd, at the Butter Market, Ipswich.

On the hill-top
above the cornfield
stands the silver wood.

At dawn the sky is rose-pink,
at noon cornflower-blue,
and at dusk poppy-red,
but always the trees are silver.

At night, when the stars and the full moon
hang above the wood,
not only the trees
but all the world is silver.

Many birds and animals
have their homes in the wood.
In the banks along its edges
live rabbits, tiny mice,
and furry moles that tunnel
through the soft earth.

In the bushes
a red fox has his lair.
And in a hole in a tree
lives a round-eyed owl.
Gentle deer graze in the clearings.
Squirrels leap from branch to bough.

And in the middle of the wood
lives the woodman in his cottage.

The woodman is a young man
and very tall.
His eyes are clear and blue,
his face berry-brown,
and his arms and hands
thick and strong.

His cottage is small
with a low door.
It has a crooked chimney,
a mossy roof,
a rain barrel at one end,
and a pile of logs near the other.

The woodman lives alone in the cottage
but he is not lonely in the wood,
for the birds and animals
are his friends.

In the spring,
when the birches turn soft green
and patches of primroses
appear in the grass,
the woodman nails birdhouses
to the trees nearest the cottage.
Bright little chickadees
come to look
and bob in and out of the holes.

When nest-building begins,
the woodman leaves hay
and moss by his door,
and pieces of wool
pulled from an old scarf.

When the baby birds are born
he puts food on the window-sill.
But the parent birds
are not the only visitors.
Every morning
a bushy-tailed squirrel
also comes for food,
peers in at the window,
and knocks with his nose
on the pane.

Early on summer days,
the woodman walks
among the silver trees,
and meets young creatures on all sides.
Little rabbits follow through the flowers
behind their mothers' flashing white tails.
Fox cubs play on the woodland paths.
Baby birds, still begging to be fed,
flutter across the clearings.
And a fawn lies hidden
in the shadows.

One afternoon,
a family of picnickers
came to the silver wood,
and ate their lunch.
They lit a fire,
played for a while,
and then went home.

But the fire was left smoldering.

The woodman was asleep
outside his cottage.
He did not see
the column of smoke
rising above the trees.
But the mother deer smelled it,
and watched anxiously.
Little flames
ran through
the dry grass
towards
the burrows
in the banks.
The rabbits watched anxiously.
Squirrels scurried
in the trees,
and birds
flew deeper into the wood.

The woodman was still asleep.
But his old dog,
smelling the smoke,
sensed danger and barked.

At once
the woodman woke up
and rushed through the trees to the fire.

He stamped on the flames,
and beat them with branches.
As he stopped the fire in one place,
it spread in another.
All evening he fought the flames,
but at sunset
they were still burning.
As darkness spread,
a red glow still showed
at the edge of the wood.

The woodman was hot and tired.
The smoke choked him,
and his eyes were sore.
But he looked up
at the sky
and smiled.
A drop
of rain
had touched
his cheek.
Soon
trickles
began running
down his face.
And as the rain fell heavily
the flames hissed,
flickered,
and died.

Then the fire was out.
When the woodman
walked home with his dog,
the wood was quiet again.

In the autumn, the leaves
of the silver trees turn to gold.
At first only a few float down,
and lie on the path.
But, later, showers of leaves fall
with each breath of wind.

Toadstools
make magic circles
around tree-stumps.
Ferns, once green,
turn copper-color.

This is a busy season
for the woodman.
The clearings have to be planted
with young fir trees.
Old birches
have to be felled and burned.
All day long
the air is filled
with the smell of burning logs,
and blue smoke drifts
among shafts of sunlight.
Early in the evenings
mists appear in the hollows
and along the paths,
and the owl cries eerily
on her lonely flight.

When the first storms
of winter come,
the wind gathers up the leaves
and whirls them through the air.
The rain
beats on the cottage roof
and against the window-panes,
making the drain-pipe gurgle
and the rain barrel overflow.

Then one morning,
the grass is white
with glistening frost,
and the air is sharp.
A hedgehog,
who has spent the autumn
searching for slugs and beetles
among tree-roots
and the stones of an old wall,
decides he has delayed long enough.
That evening,
at the bottom of a sheltered bank,
he rolls himself
in a blanket of leaves,
and, snug and warm,
begins his long winter's sleep.

Mice from the cornfield
have stored heaps of grain
in their burrows,
and they, too,
curl up to sleep.
Like the squirrels,
they will wake up now and again
on warmer winter days.

But the fox,
the deer,
the rabbits,
and the birds
will not go to sleep.
They will have to spend
the long winter
searching,
searching for food.

One night,
at Christmas-time,
as the woodman
was carrying in
more logs for his fire,
a little snow
began to fall
and settled on his sleeve.

Later,
when he looked
from his bedroom window,
the yellow light
shone onto a dense curtain
of falling flakes.
But during the night

the snow suddenly stopped.
At dawn
the woodman walked in a new world,
silent,
white.

Every bough, branch and twig
was trimmed with white.
As the sun rose,
rays of pale sunshine
fell between the trees
and the snow sparkled
with dancing lights.

Even on that first day
the woodman found tracks in the snow.
The deer had dug with dainty hoofs
for grass and tender shoots,
and the fox had left an endless line of prints
through the wood
and across the empty fields.

On Christmas Eve
the woodman gathered holly boughs
laden with bright berries,
and hung them around his room.
Then he set up a fir tree
outside the cottage door.
Christmas day
many birds flew to the tree,
and a robin
sang merrily
in the green branches.

That night
the woodman sat with his dog
before a roaring fire.
From afar
the lights of his cottage
could be seen shining
through the trees.

On top of the hill,
the silver wood
lay under a starry sky,
at peace.